by Dian Curtis Regan

illustrated by Doug Cushman

Holiday House / New York

HOLIDAY HOUSE is registered in the U.S. Patent and Trademark Office.
Printed and Bound in April 2011 at Tien Wah Press, Johor Bahru, Johor, Malaysia.
The text typeface is Joel 1.
The artwork was created with pen and ink and watercolors on Lanarelle watercolor paper.
www.holidayhouse.com
First Edition
1 3 5 7 9 10 8 6 4 2

Library of Congress Cataloging-in-Publication Data
Regan, Dian Curtis.
The Snow Blew Inn / by Dian Curtis Regan ; illustrated by Doug Cushman. — 1st ed.
p. cm.
Summary: As Emma waits with excitement for her cousin Abby to arrive for a sleepover,
a snowstorm brings so many visitors to her family's inn that she and her mother give up
their own rooms, and still Abby has not appeared.
ISBN 978-0-8234-2351-4 (hardcover)
[1. Taverns (Inns)—Fiction. 2. Storms—Fiction. 3. Sleepovers—Fiction. 4. Animals—Fiction.]
I. Cushman, Doug, ill. II. Title.
PZ7.R25854Sno 2011
E—dc22
2010029444

For Kelci Rane Potts
—D. C. R.

For Erzsi and all her
little hens in ink
—D. C.

Emma sees dark clouds boiling above mountain peaks. Snow is coming to the Snow Blew Inn!

Is Cousin Abby coming down the trail?
"Not yet, not yet," calls Mr. Owl.
"Storm, storm!"

"Abby and I will build a snowcat,"
Emma tells the frosty windowpane,
"and make a snow cave just for two."

Upstairs in her cold and tiny room, Emma dresses her doll in winter clothes. She hopes Abby brings her doll too.

Emma hangs up a banner she painted
all by herself.

She checks again for Abby, even
though Mr. Owl is keeping watch.

Mama makes the rounds with
extra blankets and firewood.
Emma helps.

Snow begins to fall as guests arrive.
And arrive. And arrive.

The Snow Blew Inn fills up quickly.
Emma hangs the No Vacancy sign.

Time to light the inn's lamps.

Emma sets a small table with two bowls
and the prettiest lace napkins.
Mama serves her famous winter stew.

The table fills up as more guests arrive.
Mama tells these cold and hungry travelers
she will squeeze them in.

Emma eats supper
alone at the little table.

After dinner, guests gather in the parlor.
Emma puts an empty chair next to hers for Abby.

A baby cries. His father hushes him with a
round of "Sleep, Little Bear." Grandmother Rabbit
joins in. Then Miss Deer.

But not Emma. She won't feel like singing until
Abby comes.

More travelers arrive, tracking in snow.
They shiver in front of the fire.

"I want to go home," a baby raccoon wails.
"*shh-shh*," says his grandpapa.

Mama gives away her room
to the Squirrel family.

Wind howls, splattering snowflakes against the windows.

Where are Abby and her mama? Are they cold and wet and hungry?

"The Snow Blew Inn is full, full, full,"
Mama says as the guests settle in for the night.

Emma bundles up and goes outside to look
for Abby. She sees the Fox family looking at
the No Vacancy sign. "My mama says the inn
is full, full, full."

Emma thinks about Abby and her mama,
out in the blizzard with no place to stay.
"I guess there's one more room,
but it's tiny and cold."

Emma helps carry bags to her room.
"It's perfect!" says Mrs. Fox, yet Emma knows
the bed is too small for two. She pulls down the
banner and fetches her doll.

Mama comes to greet the newest guests.
"I'm proud of you," she tells Emma.

Outside, wind hushes and the night grows calm.
"I miss Abby," Emma tells her doll.

She and Mama settle into makeshift beds in the parlor. Popcorn with extra butter makes a hard floor seem softer.

Mr. Owl taps on the window.
"Here! Here!"

Now the Snow Blew Inn is full, full, full.
Emma's sleepover has finally begun.

Father Bear's Song

Sleep, Little Bear,
in your cozy lair.
The wind may howl
and blow up a storm.
Inside you're safe.
Inside you're warm.
Sleep, Little Bear, sleep.